Hazen Memorial Library
3 Keady Way
Shirley, MA 01464
978.425.2620

WITHDRAWN

W9-ATT-325

11/30/15 B+T $16.99

I AM HENRY FINCH

For Ben Norland

Text copyright © 2015 by Alexis Deacon • Illustrations copyright © 2015 by Viviane Schwarz

All rights reserved. No part of this book may be reproduced, transmitted, or stored in an information retrieval system in any form or by any means, graphic, electronic, or mechanical, including photocopying, taping, and recording, without prior written permission from the publisher.

First U.S. edition 2015

Library of Congress Catalog Card Number 2014949717

ISBN 978-0-7636-7812-8

15 16 17 18 19 20 APS 10 9 8 7 6 5 4 3 2 1

Printed in Humen, Dongguan, China

This book was typeset in Helvetica Neue. • The illustrations were done in pen, watercolor, and fingerprints.

Candlewick Press
99 Dover Street
Somerville, Massachusetts 02144

visit us at www.candlewick.com

I Am Henry Finch

Alexis Deacon illustrated by Viviane Schwarz

CANDLEWICK PRESS

The finches lived in a great flock.
They made such a racket all day long, they
really could not hear themselves think.

Every morning, they said GOOD MORNING.

Every afternoon, they said GOOD AFTERNOON.

In the evening, they said GOOD EVENING.

At night, they said GOOD NIGHT.

In the morning, they started over.

It was always the same.
Except . . .

sometimes the Beast came.

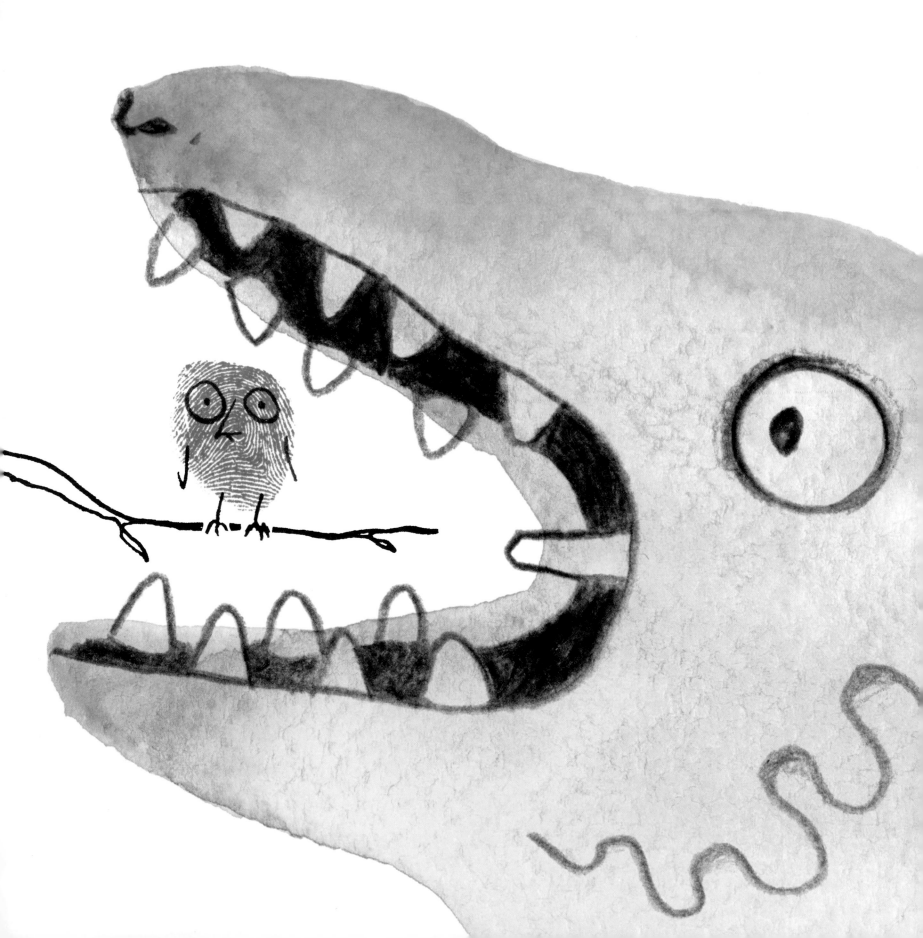

Then they would all shout,
THE BEAST, THE BEAST!

and fly as fast as they could
to the top of the nearest tree,
where they would sit and shout
until the Beast moved on.

This was the way it always was.

Until

one night

something else

happened.

A finch woke up in the dark
and the quiet.

He had a thought, and he heard it.

I AM HENRY FINCH,

he thought.

I THINK,

he thought.

He sat still and listened to his thoughts.

He had more of them.

He liked them.

AM I THE FIRST FINCH TO EVER HAVE A THOUGHT? he thought.

I COULD BE GREAT, thought Henry.

The next morning, the Beast came.

It was the time for greatness.

I AM HENRY FINCH!

screamed Henry Finch, and he dived
down straight at the Beast . . .

who ate him.

It was very dark inside
the Beast and very quiet.

I WILL LISTEN TO MY THOUGHTS,
Henry Finch said.

But they were bad thoughts.

YOU ARE A FOOL, HENRY FINCH,
he thought.

*YOU ARE NOT GREAT. YOU ARE
ONLY SOMEONE'S DINNER.*

Now Henry did not like his
thoughts at all. He tried not to think,
but what else could he do?

He thought and thought and thought.

WHO AM I? he thought.
AM I HENRY FINCH?
I AM SOMETHING, I THINK.

I AM,
he thought.

IT IS,

he thought.

Then all
his thoughts
fell silent.

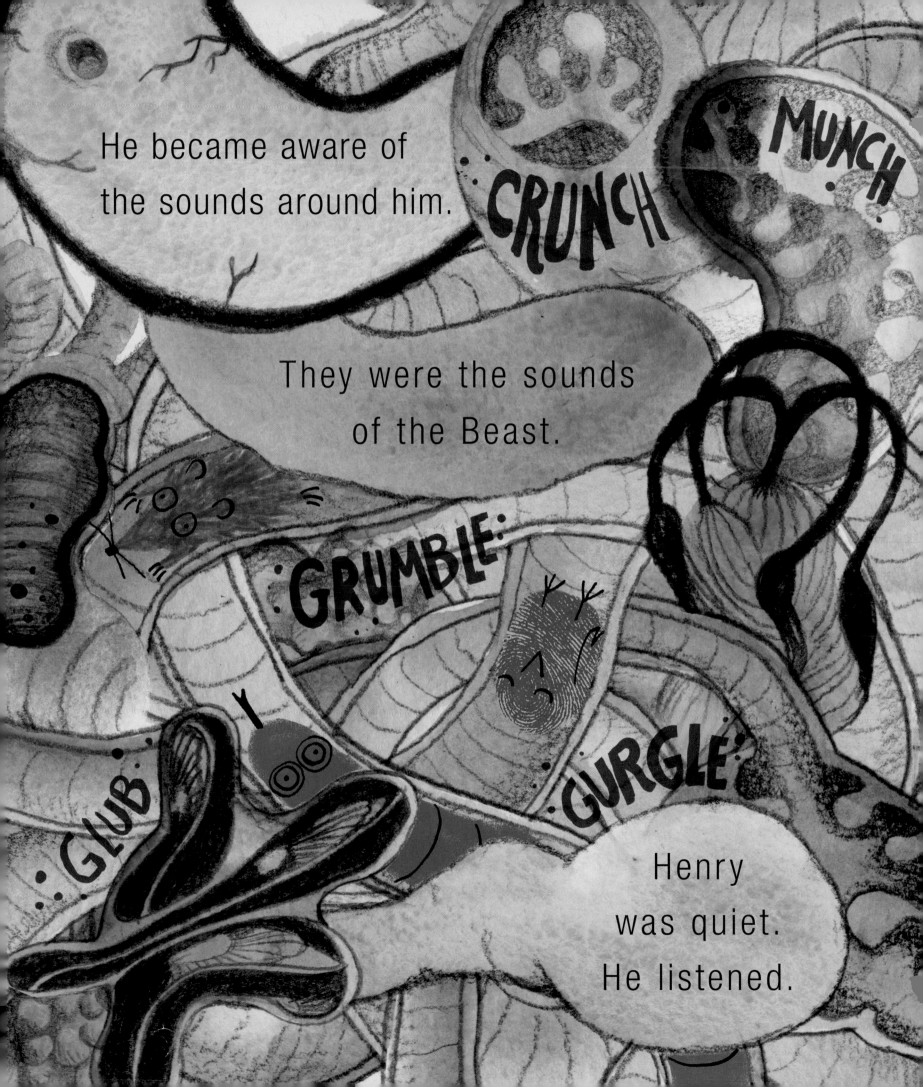

He became aware of
the sounds around him.

CRUNCH

MUNCH

They were the sounds
of the Beast.

GRUMBLE

GLUB

GURGLE

Henry
was quiet.
He listened.

He could hear the thoughts of the Beast!

GOT TO EAT.
GOT TO HUNT. GOT TO
FIND MORE FOOD.
BIG FAMILY ALL NEED
FEEDING. CRAWLING,
SWIMMING, FLYING,
WALKING . . . ANYTHING
WILL DO.

NO!
said Henry.

NO? thought the Beast.

THOSE
CREATURES
HAVE
FAMILIES
LIKE YOU,
thought Henry.

LIKE ME? thought the Beast.

*YOU WILL
EAT PLANTS
FROM NOW
ON,* thought
Henry. *THEY
HAVE PARTS
TO SPARE.*

I WILL EAT PLANTS,
thought
the
Beast.

AND NOW, thought
Henry, *YOU WILL
OPEN YOUR
MOUTH AS WIDE
AS YOU CAN AND
HOLD IT LIKE THAT
FOR A BIT.*

OPEN,

thought the beast.

Out flew Henry!

HEY! someone called
from the top of the
tree. EVERYONE!
IT'S HENRY!

GOOD MORNING,
EVERYONE, said Henry.

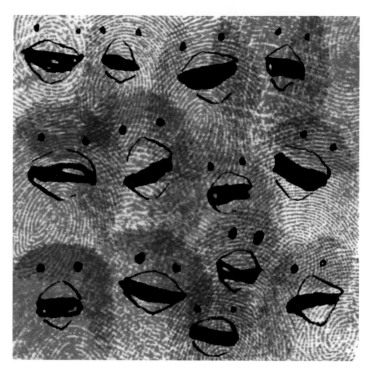

GOOD MORNING, HENRY
FINCH, said everyone.

I HAVE SOMETHING TO TELL
YOU, said Henry. BUT FIRST
YOU HAVE TO BE QUIET.

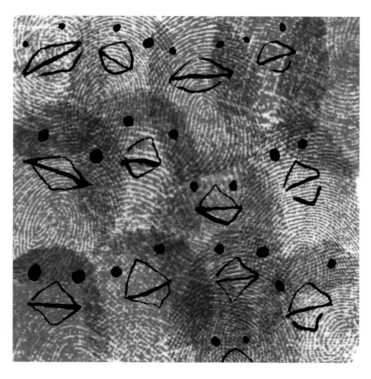

Everyone was quiet.

Henry told the finches about everything that had happened, and they listened.

When he had finished, no one moved. They stayed quiet.

Then a little voice said,

I HAVE HAD A THOUGHT.
GOOD-BYE, EVERYONE.
I WILL COME BACK.

One by one, the finches flew off.
WE WILL COME BACK,
they called behind them.

Henry looked up at them.
He smiled a finch smile.

GREAT!

thought Henry.

Hazen Memorial Library
3 Keady Way
Shirley, MA 01464
978.425.2620